Whiff Erik
and the
Great Green Thing

THE GOOSE PIMPLE BAY · SAGAS ·

Whiff Erik and the Great Green Thing

Karen Wallace

Illustrated by Nigel Baines

A & C Black • London

For Caspian

First published 2007 by
A & C Black Publishers Ltd
38 Soho Square, London, W1D 3HB

www.acblack.com

Text copyright © 2007 Karen Wallace
Illustrations copyright © 2007 Nigel Baines

The rights of Karen Wallace and Nigel Baines to be identified as
the author and illustrator of this work have been asserted by them in
accordance with the Copyrights, Designs and Patents Act 1988.

ISBN 978-0-7136-7993-9

A CIP catalogue for this book is available from the British Library.

This book is produced using paper that is made from wood
grown in managed, sustainable forests. It is natural, renewable and
recyclable. The logging and manufacturing processes conform
to the environmental regulations of the country of origin.

Printed and bound in Great Britain by MPG Books Limited.

Chapter One

Whiff Erik reached into his big leather bag. First thing that morning it had been full of carrots. Now, even though the sun was barely half-way up the sky, the bag was almost empty.

He stuffed another carrot into his mouth and began to chomp nervously.

A scrawny crow hopped down from a branch and peered at him.

"So what if I eat too many carrots?" snapped Whiff Erik, guiltily. "It's none of your business." As he waved his arm at the crow, his carrot-coloured skin glowed in the sunshine.

The crow let out a startled squawk and flew off as fast as it could. Vikings were bad enough but carrot-coloured ones were really scary.

Whiff Erik groaned. Ever since his mother, Ma Moosejaw, and his father, Chief Thunderstruck, had left him to look after Goose Pimple Bay, he knew he had started to act more and more strangely. Even his dear wife, Fernsilver, who was the sweetest, kindest person in the world couldn't help.

Every morning, he got out of bed before dawn and sneaked through the

Great Hall. He didn't want to wake up any of the other Vikings, who were asleep under the table.

Then he opened the huge wooden door and tiptoed outside to the vegetable shed, where the carrots were stored. After he had stuffed himself with at least six of the biggest ones he could find, he filled up his leather bag and set off on his daily weeding mission.

To Whiff Erik, a weeding mission meant crawling through every row of every vegetable garden he had planted in Goose Pimple Bay.

It was hard, tiring work growing vegetables – especially carrots – so he had to keep his strength up. And that meant eating carrots. Whiff Erik groaned again. Everything in his life seemed to be connected, and to go round and round and round.

He stared down at his bright-orange hands as they rested on his bright-orange knees. Maybe things would have been better if his mean, horrible older brother, Spike Carbuncle, had taken over running Goose Pimple Bay. But that hadn't happened because Ma Moosejaw hadn't liked Spike's disgusting wife, Fangtrude, and luckily for her, Fangtrude had no plans to stay anyway. In her country, the men went to live with their wife's family, so Spike Carbuncle had left, too.

"There you are," said a voice that sounded as sweet as a babbling brook. "I've been looking for you everywhere." Fernsilver appeared from behind a row of green beans and sat down beside Whiff Erik. "Have you had any breakfast?"

"Just a few carrots," muttered Whiff Erik, trying not to meet his wife's big, blue eyes. "I, uh, got up early because I didn't want to wake anyone."

Fernsilver stood up. "You mean, you got up early so you could sneak through the Great Hall while everyone was asleep and fill up your carrot bag."

Whiff Erik bit his lip and said nothing.

"Exactly how many carrots have you eaten this morning?" she demanded.

Whiff Erik looked guilty. It was impossible to lie to his wife. Those big, blue eyes of hers could see right into your brain. Although lately he was beginning to think they seemed a bit bossy, too.

"Thirty one," whispered Whiff Erik. His fingers closed around the wet stub of a carrot that was lying on the ground. "I mean, thirty one and a half."

"And how many vegetable gardens have you weeded?"

Whiff Erik's eyes brightened. Maybe Fernsilver wasn't going to tell him off after all. "The big, round one by the barn, the square one by the pig sty, the funny-shaped one by the orchard and the long, thin one by the meadow." He swallowed proudly. "Now I'm going to start on the ones on the other side of the Great Hall." As he spoke, he forgot himself and stuffed the stub of carrot in his mouth.

Fernsilver looked down at the ground. There had been a time when she spent her days humming happy tunes, looking after her goats, baking bread and smiling a lot. Now everything had changed and she could hardly remember the nice person she had been when she first arrived at Goose Pimple Bay.

As Fernsilver stared at her husband's orange arms and orange face – even his eyeballs looked orange – and watched him eat another carrot, something suddenly snapped inside her. "You're CRAZY!" she shouted. "And you're driving everyone else absolutely MAD!"

Whiff Erik stared in astonishment. Fernsilver had never shouted at him before. "I don't understand," he spluttered. "I know I eat too many carrots and I know I spend too much time weeding but what's that got to do with anyone else?"

12

"Don't you remember the new law you announced last week?" cried Fernsilver. "Now everyone in Goose Pimple Bay has to eat ten bowls of vegetables every day. And anyone caught finishing their meat before they have eaten their vegetables has to eat ten more bowls of vegetables."

Whiff Erik pulled a face. "Vegetables are good for people," he muttered.

"NOT THAT GOOD!" Fernsilver screamed at the top of her voice. And then she did something else she had never done before. She picked up Whiff Erik's bag of carrots and dumped it over his head.

That night Whiff Erik went to bed early because he had a headache.

"You'll be better in the morning," said Fernsilver as she shut the bedroom door. But she didn't believe it.

As soon as she got back to the Great Hall, for the first time ever she banged her mug on the table.

Everyone looked serious, because everyone knew Fernsilver was worried about Whiff Erik. And so were they. Even the fire-breathing lizard that Whiff Erik had brought back from one of his expeditions couldn't manage more than a few puffs of luke-warm smoke.

"What are we going to do?" asked Slime Fungus, who was Whiff Erik's best friend. "He's not himself. He really isn't. Yesterday I saw him weeding the vegetable garden with his teeth."

"Perhaps he should stop gardening," suggested one Viking.

"And give up vegetables," added another.

"He'd never do it," said Fernsilver. "Besides, vegetables aren't the real problem. The problem is his mind."

Everyone looked uncomfortable. Was it possible that Fernsilver wanted someone to chop off Whiff Erik's head?

"What I mean," said Fernsilver, patiently, "is that I think Whiff Erik has turned loopy."

A nod went round the table. After all, what sort of chief would force his people to eat ten bowls of vegetables a day?

"Whiff Erik's gone *soft*." Axehead, a friend of Spike Carbuncle, swallowed his beer and pushed aside his bowl of uneaten cabbage. "Send him to sea on the *Dithering Duck*. *Real* Viking chiefs go on

16

expeditions and bring things back home. He should do the same. If he doesn't come back, he's no good anyway."

Fernsilver narrowed her big, blue eyes. The *Dithering Duck* was Whiff Erik's boat and it was true, it hadn't left Goose Pimple Bay for a long time. An expedition was a good idea. It would give Whiff Erik some time to relax and, best of all, there were no carrots at sea, so he would *have* to stop eating them.

"That's a brilliant plan!" she cried and, leaning forward, Fernsilver planted a kiss on Axehead's low, hairy forehead. "You're very kind and very clever."

Poor Axehead went bright red. No one, not even his mother, had ever called him kind or clever before.

"Whiff Erik will leave tomorrow morning!" announced Fernsilver. She raised her mug. "Let's drink to a successful expedition!"

Then there was a great roar and a gurgle as all the Vikings swallowed their beer in one gulp.

Chapter Two

The *Dithering Duck* was delighted to see Whiff Erik when he arrived at the harbour the next morning at dawn. He had been feeling lonely.

Since Spike Carbuncle had sailed off in his own boat, the *Stealthy Stoat*, the poor Duck had been left all on his own. And, even though the two boats hated each other and argued all the time, at least it was something to do. Now the *Dithering Duck* was sick of spending his time listening to seagulls squawking or seals barking or trying to guess what was making *sploshing* noises in the water at night.

"Welcome aboard!" quacked the *Dithering Duck*. "Where's it to be? Somewhere near? Somewhere far? How about a tropical paradise with sparkling white beaches and a fringe of palm trees?"

Whiff Erik flung down the bag that Fernsilver had handed him before he left the Great Hall. He knew she had packed it so he couldn't sneak in any carrots.

"I don't care where we go, Duck," he said in a miserable voice, as he untied the rope from the quay. "They all want to get rid of me. Fernsilver wouldn't even come to say goodbye. Let's just get out of here."

The Duck cocked his head. "Like that is it? Righty ho! No worries! Leave it to me!"

And sure enough, the Duck was true to his word. An hour later, they were sailing over a bright-blue sea and Goose Pimple Bay was no more than a smudge on the horizon.

❋❋❋

A week later, Whiff Erik was sick to death of sailing about in the sunshine, stopping at rocky islands and looking for something to take back home. He couldn't find anything he liked and all night he dreamt of carrots and weeding vegetable gardens.

"What am I going to do, Duck?" he asked.

"Drink sea water," quacked the *Dithering Duck*. "It's the only way."

"But that drives you crazy," replied Whiff Erik. "What good would that do?"

"You're crazy already!" quacked the Duck. "It's worth a try."

So, for another week, Whiff Erik drank lots of sea water and very soon he stopped dreaming of carrots and weeding vegetables. In fact, he stopped dreaming altogether. Mostly he sat in the bottom of the *Dithering Duck* and howled.

"Better," quacked the Duck, kindly. "Much better. Soon you'll be ready to go home."

✳✳✳

That evening, a huge fog rolled across the sea and everything turned grey and nasty. In fact, it was so foggy that Whiff Erik couldn't even see his hand in front of his face.

"What are we going to do now, Duck?" asked Whiff Erik. "We can't possibly sail in this fog. We'll bang into something."

"Stop worrying!" quacked the Duck. "The salt water did the trick, didn't it? Have I ever let you down?"

At that moment, there was a loud *bang* and the sound of terrible swearing. The swear words were so bad, even the fog seemed to turn purple and Whiff Erik was sure he could smell something like rotten eggs in the air.

However, as the yelling continued and the stink got worse, Whiff Erik's heart leapt! "Spike!" he shouted into the fog. "Spike! Is that you?"

A moment later, Spike Carbuncle's voice yelled back. "Of course it is, you lard-headed moron! Who else would it be?"

But before Whiff Erik could reply, there was another *bang* and an equally nasty voice snarled. "You stupid bird-brain! Get out of my sea!"

"Don't call me bird-brain, you daft weasel," squawked the Duck furiously. But even as he squawked, his feathers went all tingly. It was his old enemy, the *Stealthy Stoat*! "Stoat!" he cried. "What are you doing here?"

"We're lost, dumb fluff!" yelled the *Stealthy Stoat*.

"Do something about it, whale breath!" bellowed Spike Carbuncle, to no one in particular.

It didn't matter that his brother hadn't bothered to say hello or that neither he nor the *Stealthy Stoat* had once used the words "please" or "thank you". Whiff Erik threw Spike Carbuncle a rope and the *Dithering Duck* towed the *Stealthy Stoat* through the fog.

Two hours later, they were tied up safely in a rocky cove. The fog had lifted and stars twinkled in the sky.

"So what are you doing out here on your own?" asked Whiff Erik, as he and Spike Carbuncle sat around a fire, eating fried fish and drinking beer.

Spike Carbuncle stuffed a whole fish in his mouth. "I was going to ask you the same question."

"I'm on an expedition." Whiff Erik shrugged. "Your friend Axehead said I had to bring something home."

"What for?" asked Spike Carbuncle.

"Because I'm a Viking chief," replied Whiff Erik.

Spike Carbuncle rolled his eyes. "Huh," he said. "Some chief. You're a weedy, wet gardener. And you look like you've been in the sun for months."

"That's the carrots," explained Whiff Erik.

"What?"

"It's a long story."

"Tell me."

So, after Whiff told Spike about his problem with eating carrots and weeding vegetable gardens and how drinking salt water had sorted him out, Spike told Whiff why he was on a boat in the middle of the sea. It only took one word.

Fangtrude.

"She's *disgusting*!" cried Spike. "I mean *really awful*. And her tribe is even worse! I know I'm pretty foul, but they live in caves like *animals*!" His voice dropped. "In fact, I think she *is* part animal."

Whiff Erik said nothing. He remembered the moment he had first come across Fangtrude at sea and she had climbed into his boat. She had looked just like a stinking, wet wolverine.

Spike coughed to hide a gulp. "I couldn't stand it any more, Whiff. I really missed the Great Hall and the fire-breathing lizard and, well, I really missed Goose Pimple Bay."

Whiff Erik's eyes were as big as saucers. "So you're running away?"

"Yup!" Spike Carbuncle scrambled to his feet. "And I'm never going back! *Never!*" As he jumped up, something fell out his tunic and landed on the sand.

It was a purple bean with shiny, green stripes. Whiff Erik had never seen anything like it before.

"What's *that*?" he asked.

"I don't know," replied Spike Carbuncle.

He stuffed another fish in his mouth. "But it was inside a leather pouch Fangtrude always wore."

"You mean you *stole* her pouch?" asked Whiff Erik, jumping to his feet.

Spike Carbuncle nodded. "I thought there was gold in it."

Whiff Erik held the strange bean in his hand. "This is some kind of seed. Can I have it?"

"Help yourself."

Whiff Erik was delighted. At last he had something to take back to Goose Pimple Bay! "Come on," he cried. "The *Dithering Duck* knows how to follow the stars. Let's go home!"

Chapter Three

When Whiff Erik walked through the door of the Great Hall with Spike Carbuncle beside him, everyone let out a great roar of delight. Because even though Spike Carbuncle could be mean and horrible, he was still part of Goose Pimple Bay and most of the Vikings had forgotten how unpleasant he really was.

Slime Fungus handed Whiff Erik a mug of beer. "What happened?" he asked. "Tell us everything."

"Yeah!" yelled Axehead. "What did you bring us?" He turned and punched Spike Carbuncle playfully on the head.

Spike punched him back, and they immediately began to fight.

Whiff Erik ignored them both and walked into the middle of the Great Hall. Then he told all the other Vikings how he had sailed around for weeks with only sea water to drink and how he had found Spike Carbuncle and rescued him and finally how he had brought them back a very strange bean.

Everyone agreed that while the bean was pretty boring, the important thing was it seemed like their chief was back to normal again.

Fernsilver was delighted to see the difference in Whiff Erik. He hadn't reached for a carrot once and his skin looked only faintly tanned. The sea water must have done the trick.

It was only later, when Whiff Erik and Fernsilver were alone, that things began to go wrong. The problem was that Whiff Erik was determined to plant the bean that night and Fernsilver was just as determined to throw it in the fire.

"Don't you understand," said Fernsilver. "That bean can only bring trouble. You said yourself that Spike stole it from Fangtrude. And it's wrong to steal."

"But I've never seen anything like it before," said Whiff Erik. "At least let me find out what kind of plant it is."

"No," said Fernsilver.

"Please," said Whiff Erik.

"No!" repeated Fernsilver. And she

grabbed the bean from Whiff Erik's hands and tried to throw it on the fire.

Quick as a flash, Whiff Erik grabbed it back and before Fernsilver could stop him, he threw the bean out of the window, where it landed in a patch of warm, wet mud.

As they stood glaring at each other, the strangest noise floated through the window. It was a cross between a growl and a low, nasty chuckle.

The next morning, Whiff Erik woke up to find the room bathed in a dark, green light. At first he thought someone had put a green blanket over the window. Then he saw that the window was covered with leaves, which were blocking out the daylight. Not only that, a long leafy stem was spreading slowly down the wall and creeping across the floor.

Whiff Erik clutched his forehead and tried not to scream. He knew immediately that this strange green thing had grown from the bean. Fernsilver had been right. He should have thrown it in the fire. And then another idea came into his mind and he went sweaty all over.

What if the strange green thing kept on growing? It would destroy Goose Pimple Bay! The more he thought of it, the more he wanted to eat a carrot. It was terrible.

"No! No! No!" screamed Whiff Erik to himself. Then he jumped out of bed and grabbed his trusty axe. He had to chop down the plant. NOW!

But when he ran around the side of the Great Hall, to his horror, Spike Carbuncle was half-way up the trunk and about to disappear into a mass of clinging, green leaves.

"Come back, Spike," yelled Whiff Erik "I'm going to chop it down."

At that moment, there was a great growling sound and a monstrous green face appeared in the leaves. It had sharp green teeth, beady green eyes and a face like a lumpy green root.

"I am the Great Green Thing of Gristledom!" it bellowed. A leafy branch like an angry arm swept Whiff Erik off his feet. "*No one* chops me down!"

To Whiff Erik's astonishment, Spike Carbuncle began to climb back down as fast as he could. "Gristledom is Fangtrude's island," he yelled. "Quick! Get it with your axe!"

But it was too late! In front of their eyes, the Great Green Thing suddenly tripled in size.

No axe could ever go through it now.

Spike Carbuncle dropped to the ground beside him. "What are we going to do?" he whispered in a terrified voice.

"YOU WILL DO WHAT YOU ARE TOLD!" yelled the Great Green Thing. The eyes narrowed and looked cunning. "You have three chances to make a wish. If you make the right one, I will disappear. If you make the wrong one..." A roar shook the air. "I WILL CRUSH THE GREAT HALL AND DESTROY GOOSE PIMPLE BAY!"

"So what's the right wish?" asked Whiff Erik.

"Don't ask stupid questions!" yelled the Great Green Thing. "You have three chances and that's it!"

Chapter Four

"I *told* you not to plant that stupid seed!" Fernsilver was with the other Vikings and she was looking very, very cross. "Now what are we going to do?"

"We've got three wishes," began Whiff Erik but then he noticed that Spike Carbuncle had disappeared. "Where's Spike?"

Fernsilver rolled her eyes and pointed half-way up the tangle of green leaves. Spike Carbuncle was climbing as fast as he could.

"I've got a wish!" he shouted.

"What is it?" demanded the Great Green Thing.

"I wish you would go back to where you came from," shouted Spike Carbuncle.

"Impossible!"

"Why?" shouted Spike Carbuncle.

"Because you took me away in the first place! Now I can never go back there, *ever*." And with that he shook a great green branch and Spike Carbuncle fell through the leaves like a lump of rock!

All the Vikings watched as Spike Carbuncle bounced once, then lay still on the ground.

"Spike!" yelled Axehead. "Speak to me, bull brain!"

But Spike said nothing and as everyone watched, he went whiter and whiter and the ends of his fingers began to twitch.

Whiff Erik let out a howl of despair. He had only just brought his brother home and, even though he was as mean and nasty as ever, it was better than having no brother at all. "I want Spike back!" he wailed.

"Is that wish number two?" asked the Great Green Thing.

"Yes!" cried Whiff Erik.

"What about a lifetime's supply of carrots?" whispered the Great Green Thing in a horrible, tempting voice.

"No!" cried Whiff Erik. "I want my brother back. I will never eat another carrot again in my life!"

"Done!" cried the Great Green Thing. "Now you have a day to make your last wish. After that…"

All the Vikings watched in horror as the Great Green Thing lifted a great green claw-like finger and dragged it across its great green throat!

***

Deep in a cave on the island of Gristledom, Fangtrude stirred and opened one blood-shot eye. She could tell from the small circle of light at the end of the rocky tunnel that it was daytime but she had no idea how long she had been asleep. As Spike Carbuncle had guessed, Fangtrude *was* part animal. A small part of her was wolverine, which meant she had a truly terrible temper, and had been known to snarl and bite. Also, she could sleep very deeply for days.

Now Fangtrude opened her other eye. Usually Spike was somewhere at arm's length but as she felt around in the shadows, she realised she was alone. Then her hand went to her waist and she let out a howl of fury. Her leather pouch was gone! And there was only one person who could have taken it.

Fangtrude gathered up some bones that still had bits of meat on them and put them into a sack. Then she crawled quickly down the rocky tunnel and out of the cave. Beyond the pebbly shore, the sea was calm and, just as she had expected, the *Stealthy Stoat* was nowhere to be seen.

Fangtrude dragged a log down to the water and began to paddle out to sea. She knew where she would find Spike Carbuncle. It was the bean she was worried about.

It had been given to her by an old wolverine witch many years before. At the time, the witch had warned Fangtrude to keep the bean safe and not plant it unless she was prepared for the very worst or, if she was incredibly lucky, the very best.

Since Fangtrude didn't believe in luck, she had never done anything with the bean. She kept it in her special pouch because it was the only thing that anyone had ever given her. As she paddled through the night, Fangtrude kept asking herself the same question: *What if someone had planted the bean?*

✳✳✳

Whiff Erik never thought he would hate the colour green. Now, as he and Spike Carbuncle hacked their way along the beach through a jungle of huge, clinging leaves, he made a promise to himself that he would give up gardening for a year.

At last they reached the harbour.

"Look, Duck," said Whiff Erik as he chopped through the rope that tied the boat to the shore. "If you don't go to sea, you'll be crushed by the Great Green Thing."

"But I've never sailed anywhere on my own," squawked the *Dithering Duck*. "You've always been with me."

"Don't be silly," replied Whiff Erik. "You're a boat. You know how to sail."

"But I can't leave you!" quacked the Duck, desperately. "Uh, you might need my help!"

Out of the corner of his eye, the *Dithering Duck* saw Spike Carbuncle trying to push the *Stealthy Stoat* away from the harbour with a pole. It was obvious the *Stealthy Stoat* was even more terrified.

"Look, Duck," said Whiff Erik, again. "If you want to help, look after the *Stealthy Stoat*. We both know that he can't really sail, and you two might have to save us."

The *Dithering Duck* turned to where Spike Carbuncle was swearing and waving his arms at his boat. "Go away, you stupid, stinking stoat! I hate you! I never want to see you again!"

But that didn't work either. The *Stealthy Stoat* wouldn't budge.

"I'll sort out that silly stoat," quacked the *Dithering Duck*. "He can never resist a bet." And before Whiff Erik could reply, he sailed away.

Five minutes later, Whiff Erik stood with Spike Carbuncle and watched as the *Stealthy Stoat* and *Dithering Duck* raced out of the harbour side by side.

Whiff Erik smiled to himself. The *Dithering Duck* was getting smarter all the time.

"Now what are we going to do?" muttered Spike Carbuncle, as the two brothers hacked a path back to the Great Hall. "This is all your fault! You should never have planted that stupid bean."

"And you should never have stolen Fangtrude's pouch," snapped Whiff Erik. "I can't believe I wasted a wish bringing you back. I should have left you lying on the ground."

Spike Carbuncle opened his mouth to reply but it filled up with leaves before he had time.

There was a *crunch* of broken branches and suddenly the other Vikings appeared with Fernsilver.

"The Great Green Thing is crushing the Great Hall!" cried Fernsilver. "We've got one hour left to make our last wish!"

"But what if we get it wrong?" wailed Slime Fungus. "Goose Pimple Bay will be destroyed! Remember the way he dragged his awful green finger across his throat?"

Everyone remembered.

"It's up to you, Whiff Erik," cried Fernsilver. "You're our chief. You've got to make the last wish."

At first Whiff Erik felt sick. Then he thought of his mother, Ma Moosejaw, with her long, lumpy nose and the steely look in her velvety, brown eyes. Suddenly he knew what to do.

"We'll have a meeting around the table in the Great Hall," announced Whiff Erik. "Everyone will write down a wish on a bit of animal skin and put it into the old war helmet with the horns." He paused. "Then *someone* will pick a wish out."

For a moment the only noise you could hear was the steady sound of leaves growing. Then Fernsilver turned to her husband with a puzzled face. "I don't understand," she said. As she spoke, she could see the other Vikings were just as confused. "What good will *that* do?"

But for the first time in his life, Whiff Erik felt completely in control. "Anyone got a better idea?" he asked.

Nobody did.

Chapter Five

By the time the Vikings reached the Great Hall, it looked like one huge pile of leaves.

Eventually they sat down in their places at the long table. Fernsilver handed out bits of animal skin and lumps of charcoal to write with.

"How are we supposed to know what the right wish is?" muttered Axehead, as he stared at his bit of animal skin.

"We're not," said Whiff Erik. "Who knows what the Great Green Thing wants to hear." He shrugged and took a slurp of his beer. "All we can do is wish for what we want."

Axehead thought of Fernsilver's kiss and how she had called him kind and clever. He picked up his lump of charcoal and wrote *I wish I had a nice mother like Fernsilver.*

No sooner had Axehead put the piece of animal skin in the helmet than a horrible howl of laughter echoed down the room. And every time someone wrote out a wish, it happened again. It was as if the Great Green Thing knew what they were writing and so far no one had got it right.

***

Fangtrude sat up on her log. She couldn't believe her eyes. Goose Pimple Bay was a mass of leaves and twisting branches.

In fact, if the *Dithering Duck* and the *Stealthy Stoat* hadn't been out at sea themselves and spotted her in the water, she would have paddled straight past.

Now, neither the *Dithering Duck* nor the *Stealthy Stoat* liked Fangtrude one little bit but, perhaps because they too had some animal in them, both boats realised the same thing – Fangtrude was the only one who could save Goose Pimple Bay from the Great Green Thing. So, instead of knocking over Fangtrude's log, they sailed up on either side and towed her to shore as quickly as possible.

As Fangtrude ran down the hacked-out path to the Great Hall, her heart began to hammer. Even though one part of her wanted to bite off Spike Carbuncle's head for stealing her pouch, the other part knew she missed him. She also realised that someone must have planted the bean. How else could Goose Pimple Bay be completely covered in leaves?

She remembered the words of the wolverine witch. If the bean was planted, she had to be prepared for the very worst, unless she was incredibly lucky and got the very best.

Fangtrude ran faster. She was sure the very worst was about to happen.

✳✳✳

"Time's up!" roared the Great Green Thing as it hung upside down in the doorway of the Great Hall. Its giant green leaves had covered the walls, the roof and then spread over the floor. Sure enough, the Great Hall was about to be crushed! "I want your last wish – NOW!"

Fernsilver banged her mug on the table. "Who's going to pick the wish from the helmet?"

"Not me!" yelled every voice around the table.

"I'll do it!" said Whiff Erik. "I am chief, after all."

Everyone held their breath as Whiff Erik stood up and walked over to the helmet.

"You've got five seconds!" bellowed the Great Green Thing.

Whiff Erik closed his eyes.

"FIVE!" yelled the Great Green Thing. It wrapped a leaf around Fernsilver's wrist.

Whiff Erik took a deep breath.

"FOUR!" yelled the Great Green Thing. It twisted a stem around Slime Fungus's neck.

Whiff Erik held out his dirty hand.

"THREE!" yelled the Great Green Thing. It climbed up Axehead's leg.

Whiff Erik stirred up the pieces of animal skin in the helmet.

"TWO!" yelled the Great Green Thing. It poked a twig in Spike Carbuncle's ear.

Whiff Erik picked out a piece of animal skin. It said *I wish I had a nice mother like Fernsilver.*

"ONE!" yelled the Great Green Thing. There was a crunching noise as if the branches were beginning to join together over the top of the Great Hall.

Whiff Erik looked up at the doorway. There was something behind the Great Green Thing's ear. It had a face like a wolverine with two bloodshot eyes.

"Fangtrude!" he shouted in astonishment.

"Is that a wish?" asked the Great Green Thing.

Whiff Erik froze. There was something in its voice. Something like amazement or maybe it was disappointment.

Whiff Erik made a split-second decision. "Yes!" he cried. "That is my wish. I wish Fangtrude was here, right now!"

POOOF! There was a great explosion of green gas and, the next moment, all the leaves, all the stems and all the branches disappeared.

The Great Green Thing had gone!

Everyone began shouting at the same time. Spike Carbuncle jumped to his feet and threw his arms around his brother's neck! "You've saved Goose Pimple Bay!" he cried. "How did you know what to wish for?" Then he followed Whiff Erik's astonished gaze and saw Fangtrude standing shyly by the door.

At first Spike Carbuncle thought he was seeing things. *Fangtrude? Shy? Impossible!*

"Spike!" cried Fangtrude.

All through the night, as she has paddled in the water, Fangtrude had thought long and hard about how she had behaved on her island. She knew now that there was no need to live in a cave and that they didn't have to only eat bones. She raced towards her husband.

"I know I've behaved like an animal," blurted out Fangtrude. "But please take me back. I'll be different this time."

"She means a different kind of animal," muttered Axehead.

But Spike Carbuncle wasn't listening. He looked at his wife's sharp, hairy face and they fell into each other's arms just as they had done when they first met.

Suddently Spike froze. "I'm not going to live in a cave," he said. "And I'm not chewing any more old bones. I want to stay here in Goose Pimple Bay."

And, to his astonishment, Fangtrude didn't bite or snarl or swear. She just smiled another shy smile and said, "OK."

Whiff Erik went up to Fernsilver and took her hand. "I'm sorry, too," he whispered. "I should have listened to you. I should have thrown that stupid bean on the fire."

"I should never have dumped those…" Fernsilver paused. "Those you-know-whats over your head."

"And I should never have—" but Whiff Erik didn't want to think about the past any more. He gave Fernsilver a quick kiss on the cheek and then turned back to the room.

"Vikings of Goose Pimple Bay," cried Whiff Erik. "The Great Green Thing, uh, the Great Green Thing…" then the strangest words came into his head. "The Great Green Thing threatened us with the very worst but luckily we have been given the very best." He turned and a big smile spread across his face. "Spike and Fangtrude are here to stay!"

At that, all the Vikings cheered. After all, everyone deserves a second chance.

"Here's to our chief!" they roared. "He has saved the day!"

Then everyone raised their mugs and drank a toast to Whiff Erik, the best chief ever!

Ma Moosejaw Means Business

"That's a brilliant plan! Let's do it..."

Ma Moosejaw wants to leave
Goose Pimple Bay with her husband.
But both their sons are useless. Who will look
after things when they are gone? There's
only one thing for it — the sons must find
brides. Whoever returns with the best one
will rule Goose Pimple Bay. The other will
be banished to the forest for ever...

**The first hilarious adventure in
The Goose Pimple Bay Sagas**

Available Now!